D1482668

AFTER THE FLOOD

Arthur Geisert

Houghton Mifflin Company

Boston   1994

For Paul and Darlene Fahrenkrog

Library of Congress Cataloging-in-Publication Data

Geisert, Arthur.
  After the flood / by Arthur Geisert.
    p.   cm.
  Summary: After surviving the Flood, Noah and his family settle in
a sheltered valley with the animals they have saved and begin the
glorious experience of repopulating the Earth.
    ISBN 0-395-66611-2
    1. Noah (Biblical figure)—Juvenile fiction.   [1. Noah (Biblical
figure)—Fiction.]   I. Title.
PZ7.G2724Af   1994   93-758
[E]—dc20   CIP
                             AC

Printed in the United States of America

HOR   10   9   8   7   6   5   4   3   2   1

AFTER THE FLOOD

A long time ago there was a great flood that covered
the world. Noah built an ark and took on it two of
all the animals of the land. When the rain finally
stopped, a rainbow appeared. It was a symbol of hope.

Except for the tops of the highest mountains, water covered the earth.

When the floodwaters went down, the ark was left on Mount Ararat.

Noah, his family, and all the animals had learned to live in harmony.

But they knew they couldn't stay on Mount Ararat for long.

They decided to move to the land below.

Noah and his sons cut the ark into sections.

Trees were cut and a slide was built.

The ark was carefully moved down the mountain.

Noah, his family, and the animals all worked together.

They found a fertile valley and began preparations for planting.

The ark was turned over to make a shelter. It would become their home.

15

Seeds and shoots were planted.

Trees began to bloom.

There was time for the family.

At night, stories were read to the children and to the animals.

Crops grew.

The animals multiplied.

The people had more children.

Harvests were bountiful.

There was grain for bread and grapes for wine.

Years passed.

The people and the animals became too numerous for the valley.

Many moved away.

In time, the earth was filled again with all living things.

When it rained, Noah and his wife remembered the problems of the past.

They thought about the great flood.

But a rainbow always followed the rain.